CLASSIC STARTS™

The
Swiss Family
Robinson

*Retold from the Johann David Wyss original
by Chris Tait*

Illustrated by Jamel Akib

STERLING CHILDREN'S BOOKS

New York

STERLING CHILDREN'S BOOKS
New York

An Imprint of Sterling Publishing
387 Park Avenue South
New York, NY 10016

STERLING CHILDREN'S BOOKS and the distinctive Sterling Children's Books logo are
trademarks of Sterling Publishing Co., Inc.

ISBN 978-1-4027-3694-0

Library of Congress Cataloging-in-Publication Data

Tait, Chris.
  The Swiss family Robinson / retold from the Johann David Wyss
original ; abridged by Chris Tait ; illustrated by Jamel Akib.
    p. cm.—(Classic starts)
  Summary: An abridged version of the story that relates the fortunes
of a shipwrecked family as they imaginatively adapt to life on an
island with abundant animal and plant life.
  ISBN 978-1-4027-3694-0
  [1. Survival—Fiction. 2. Family life—Fiction. 3. Islands—Fiction.]
I. Akib, Jamel, ill. II. Wyss, Johann David, 1743–1818. Schweizerische
Robinson. III. Title.

PZ7.T1289Sw 2007
[Fic]—dc22

2006023424

Distributed in Canada by Sterling Publishing
c/o Canadian Manda Group, 165 Dufferin Street
Toronto, Ontario, Canada M6K 3H6
Distributed in the United Kingdom by GMC Distribution Services,
Castle Place, 166 High Street, Lewes, East Sussex, England BN7 1XU
Distributed in Australia by Capricorn Link (Australia) Pty. Ltd.
P.O. Box 704, Windsor, NSW 2756, Australia

For information about custom editions, special sales, and premium and corporate purchases,
please contact Sterling Special Sales at 800-805-5489 or specialsales@sterlingpublishing.com.

Printed in China
Lot#:
12 14 16 18 20 19 17 15 13
01/16

www.sterlingpublishing.com/kids

CONTENTS

CHAPTER 1

Shipwreck!

꩜

For many days, our ship was tossed in terrible storms. We were thrown about the sea and were terribly off course. Our mast was split, there were leaks all around, and water rushed in, rising quickly. Our crew gave up all hope and feared the worst. All seemed lost.

I gathered my family on the deck, and we prayed on our knees in the pelting rain. Suddenly, we heard a crew member shout out, "Land! Land!"

Our prayers had been answered. But just then, the ship wedged between two huge rocks and began to crack to pieces as water poured in from all sides.

"Lower the boats! We are lost!" yelled the captain. Our ship began to come apart. I ran to my boys and my wife and cried, "We are still above water and land is near! We can still make it!"

But as I turned, I saw that the crew had jumped into all the lifeboats. It broke my heart. How could I tell the family we had been left by our shipmates?

"Children," I shouted over the rain, "if we stay on board, after the storm we can make it to shore!" My boys were relieved, but my wife saw that I was still worried as the broken ship swayed and rolled in the waves.

"We need to find food," I yelled. "We have to stay strong for what is ahead."

As the night wore on, the waves and rain kept taking more of our ship, but we managed to stay in our cabin, above water.

We searched what was left of the ship in a panic, finding food and putting together a meal for the family.

Just then, Fritz, my oldest son, said, "Father, why don't we find something to make life jackets or float belts, and then we can all swim to the shore?"

It was a great idea. We found empty flasks and cans that we connected together to make life jackets of sorts and put them on so that we might survive if we were washed overboard. The life jackets wouldn't last for a long swim, but they might give us a moment or two more. We also found matches, knives, rope, and other useful things to carry, just in case. Fritz, Ernest, Jack, and Franz could now sleep on the broken ship, while my wife and I waited up all night, watching the storm.

Finally, when day came, we saw that the sky had begun to clear, and we woke the boys. They were surprised that the other shipmates had deserted in the lifeboats but we told them not to fear.

"But Papa!" they cried. "What has become of everyone? Are all the sailors gone? Why did they leave us?"

"We should swim to shore now," Fritz interrupted.

"I think we should build a raft and use that to get there safely," said Ernest. "These float belts may not do the trick."

"First let's search the rest of the ship to see what we can find," I answered. "Let's all meet back here with whatever we think will be useful."

My youngest son, Franz, who was only seven, went to look for fishing hooks, and my wife went to feed and comfort the animals on the ship, which were all full of fear. The rest of us set out to find what we could. Fritz went to find weapons, I looked for fresh water, and Jack went to the captain's quarters.

Jack opened the door only to be knocked over by two leaping dogs that were thrilled to be rescued. They licked him all over, and Jack climbed up on the biggest dog and proudly rode him to where I was. We joined the others and went through all we had found.

Fritz had found guns, gunpowder, and bullets. Ernest had nails, a saw, an axe, a hammer, and other tools in all of his pockets. Little Franz proudly showed us a box of fishing hooks, which I told him were the most important. My wife told us that there was a donkey, two cows, two goats, six sheep, a ram, a flock of chickens, a rooster, and two pigs on board.

Jack hit upon the idea of finding some barrels to float to shore in. They could be used to build a raft for all of us. I sawed the barrels each in half until there were eight. I joined the half-barrels together with large boards until we had built a sort of a boat of tubs. We placed rollers made from cut up poles under our boat and managed to create a lever to launch it into the water. We tied it to our broken ship and then loaded it with all of our tools, food, water, and everything else we found that might be useful. Then, we found some oars that we could row for shore with. After a busy day of preparing the raft, it was nightfall once again, and we waited tensely in the dark in hopes that another storm would not come. In the morning, we prepared to row to shore.

"Before we go," I told the boys, "make sure to leave lots of feed for the animals and make them as comfortable as you can. We may be able to come back for them in a few days." Just as we were about to leave, we heard the rooster's crow, which made us decide to gather all of the chickens to take with us.

My two eldest boys, Ernest and Fritz, took the oars. With that, it was time to head for shore. We all bravely put our lives into the little boat.

CHAPTER 2

A New World

∽

We soon glided away from the wreck and into the open sea. We all looked for land, but we kept spinning around and around until I learned how to steer the boat properly.

We had left the dogs, as we could not carry them, but as we sailed away, they jumped into the water and came after us yowling and barking. They made their way to the boat and rested their paws against it until we pulled them in, taking pity on them. We were especially glad to see the happy face of our own dog, Turk, barking at us on board.

We rowed until we came near the land. Past some cliffs, we saw a green, grassy patch among palm trees.

"I wish I'd thought to bring the telescope," I said, just as Jack pulled it from his pocket with a laugh and a twinkle in his eye. I could see through the telescope that there was a small flat beach we could land on. As we reached the shore, everyone jumped out but Franz, who was packed in a tub so tight he had to be pulled out by his mother.

The dogs ran ahead and flamingos and penguins and other birds on the beach began to shriek as they approached.

We quickly unloaded our boat, setting the chickens and rooster free to roam. We all searched madly now for a place to spend the night. Soon, we found two fallen trees, which we wedged into a frame. We draped the sailcloth we had packed in the boat around the trees, fastened it with pegs, and made ourselves a kind of tent, with an entrance we could close.

Then we sent the boys to search for moss and grass to spread out for beds while I made a fireplace near a river that ran next to the tent. We lit it with twigs and dried seaweed, filled a pot with water and food from the ship, and started to cook soup for our dinner. Fritz loaded the guns and left one with me as he went out to explore the coast beyond the river. Ernest and Jack went to look for shellfish in the shallow water along the shore.

As I worked, I suddenly heard Jack yell, and ran to him with an axe in my hands. I found that a huge lobster had clamped itself on his leg. No matter how hard he kicked, he could not get it off. I pulled it from him and Jack hit it with a stone.

"Never hit in anger, Jack," I told him. Still, I

was glad that we had another piece for our meal.

"When we cook it," said Jack, "I want a claw all for myself."

"I found oysters, but I didn't want to get wet catching them," said Ernest, who had come running up to see what the noise was about.

"Ernest," I scowled at him, "you go and get us some of those oysters for our next meal, and don't let me hear you complain again about getting your feet wet. We all have to work now to survive."

"I also found some salt in the rocks that had dried from the sea," added Ernest, trying to make good.

"Nice work," I answered. "Go bring us some. That will be wonderful."

He used a small stone to scrape some of the salt from the cracks in the rocks and brought it back in his hands, no longer worrying about getting his feet wet. As the soup boiled, we suddenly realized we had no spoons to eat with.

"We could use the oyster shells as spoons!" offered Ernest.

"A great idea, son! You lead the boys to the oysters and clean a few out."

They went into the water and Jack and Ernest brought a carefully balanced stack of the oysters back. With that, Fritz returned from his hunt with his hands behind his back.

"I didn't get anything." he said, frowning. But his brothers had seen behind his back and were pointing and yelling. Sure enough, Fritz pulled out a small pig he had caught and was hiding behind his back.

He told us what he had found on the other side of the river. The lands there were quite beautiful, with a sloping shore and a field.

"Best of all," he said, "it is filled with all sorts

of things that we can use that have floated in from the wreck. Tomorrow we will have to go and get them. We should also go back to the ship and get the animals. They can live on the other side of the river."

"Did you see any of our shipmates?" I asked.

"No," he answered, "but you should have seen the strange way this pig behaved! There were lots of them and they hopped instead of walking."

Meanwhile, Ernest had been looking at the pig closely.

"This isn't a pig," he said, "It's an agouti. I learned about them in school. Look, it has teeth like a squirrel."

"Oh," scoffed Fritz, "now you're going to prove my pig isn't a pig?"

"He's right," I said, looking closely. "It is an agouti, which is a large rodent. I have heard of them before."

While we had been talking, Jack had been prying open oysters and now handed them to us. We all gulped and tried them and were left with the shells for spoons.

As we ate, we saw that the dogs had surrounded the agouti and were about to attack it. Fritz leaped up in a rage, hit one of the dogs hard, and then threw stones after them. I quickly chased him and gave him a good talking to.

"Fritz," I said, "you have to watch your temper. You have scared the dogs, and we need them to help us. You must be calmer."

Fritz felt badly and said he was sorry. By now, it was getting dark and time for rest. The birds we had brought were all nestled around the rocks. We all settled in after a prayer. The children were surprised at how suddenly the night closed in so near to the equator. Quite quickly, we were alone in total darkness, except for our campfire. It was not quite the first night we had imagined when we set out to be farmers in a new land, as part of a colony to be started in a new world. But it was a night we would never forget in our new home.

CHAPTER 3

Attack!

The night was cold, but we managed in our tent. When we woke, Fritz and I planned to set off and learn about the land and to see if we could find other survivors. When we told the boys we were going on an adventure, they were all excited but then disappointed to not be invited.

"It's too dangerous until we know more about where we are," I explained.

"I don't know why we're looking for those people anyway," said Jack. "They left us. Why should we try to find and save them?"

"Because," I answered, "just because they were evil to us, doesn't mean we can be evil to them. They may be dying of hunger while we are not. And, besides, they might help us build a house."

Fritz and I started off on our search. As we walked on, we saw strange trees with bumps on them that I recognized as calabash trees. "These bumps," I told Fritz, "are called gourds and they are perfect for making bowls and spoons. You can even cook in them by adding hot stones to whatever is inside until it boils."

It was a simple thing that I had remembered from Columbus's travels, which I had read again and again, but Fritz thought it was amazing.

We struggled for a while but managed to cut some gourds from the trees. We filled them with sand to dry them out, and marked the spot before heading on. As we walked, I cut down what appeared to be a reed. I noticed that there was syrup running from the cut. I tasted it and realized that it was sugarcane. Fritz jumped for joy when he heard this and cut as many as he could carry. But our joy quickly turned to fear. When we came out of a clearing we were confronted by a group of monkeys. Fritz raised his gun to shoot them, but I stopped him.

"Watch this," I told him. As the monkeys sprang to the trees, I threw up a handful of stones, and the monkeys answered by shaking the trees to drop coconuts down on us.

"A live monkey in a tree is worth ten dead ones on the ground," I explained. With that, we broke open two coconuts, and ate and drank them dry. We continued to walk along, sucking on our sugarcane, and Fritz talked of how he couldn't wait to share his new discoveries with his brothers.

As we walked back to camp, our dog, Turk, suddenly appeared in the clearing and jumped into another troop of monkeys before they could get away.

We ran toward the group, but before we could get there, the dog had killed a mother monkey. Fritz ran toward the dog and pulled it away just as a baby monkey jumped into his arms and up onto his head to avoid the dog. No matter how hard Fritz shook, the baby monkey would not let go. Turk ran around us, barking frantically. Finally, I managed to coax the baby down into Fritz's arms with a small biscuit. It was no bigger than a kitten.

"Father," said Fritz, "let's keep it and raise it. It's the least we can do."

"If we do," I said, "you have to be in charge. You will be his parent now."

Fritz agreed, and with that we left the sad scene behind, our new friend sitting on Fritz's shoulder. The little monkey was afraid of Turk and would not come down for any reason. Finally, Fritz had an idea.

He called Turk and tied a leash of rope around

his neck and tied the monkey onto Turk's back as rider. Neither liked it very much, but they soon became used to it. It seemed somehow fitting after what Turk had done.

Soon we were back at camp, and were met by another dog, which we had named Juno, barking at us and the baby monkey. The boys ran up, thrilled to see the monkey and to play with him. The coconuts, gourds, and sugarcane amazed them. My wife was sad, though, that we hadn't found any other people.

Fritz began to teach the boys how to get sugar from the cane and how to drink the milk from the coconuts. My wife was happy to see our gourd bowls, and we all sat down to eat a meal of a bird that Ernest had killed.

"I think it's a penguin!" he said.

We ate the bird and then the coconuts, which we shared with our monkey, for dessert. After that, we all settled down for bed.

In the middle of the night, we awoke to the sound of a horrid and bone-chilling growling and cackling. We all sprang up to find we were under attack! Our entire camp had been set upon by wild jackals. The dogs dove out to fight the fiercest one, and Fritz and I shot into the herd until the lot scattered. It made for a long, sleepless night, and in the morning, we decided that we needed to set ourselves up properly. Sleeping in a makeshift tent was too dangerous.

First off, Fritz and I decided to go back to the ship and rescue as many animals as we could. I told my wife to fly a flag that we would be able to see so we would know they were all right while we were gone. If she took down the flag we would know she was in trouble and would come back immediately. Otherwise, we would plan on coming back the next day.

Fritz and I set off in our tub boat and got to the ship to find that although it had been wrecked on the rocks, it was still much above water and much of it was open to us.

Once on board, we built a sail on our little boat from the ship's torn sails to help us get back to shore. We saw the flag flying and knew everything was well, so we looked around and found flour, ham, vegetables, and other things such as swords, knives, and forks. It took us all day to search the entire ship. As darkness fell, we lit a fire in a large metal pan on the sloping deck and rested for the night under the stars.

The next morning, Fritz had an idea. "Let's make floating belts for all the animals and let them swim!" We tried with a sheep, and after sinking at first, it came to the surface and swam for the shore. We did this for all the animals, even the cows, which we had to strap with big barrels to keep them afloat. We sat down on the deck to watch the swimming animals and eat our lunch when suddenly Fritz yelled out, raising his gun.

We saw that a giant shark was making its way for the first of our sheep. Fritz took careful aim and shot at it, and the shark turned away, blood filling the water. Our animals were safe for now.

We sailed and rowed our loaded boat back to shore, arriving at the same time as our animals. We untied the floats and herded the animals to our family's camp. We told the family of our adventures as they told us of theirs. Ernest had found turtle eggs for supper to go with our ham, and my wife showed us the table she had made from a butter cask for us to eat on. It was a wonderful dinner indeed after such a dangerous day!

CHAPTER 4

A Home Up High

Over dinner, my wife told us what had happened while Fritz and I had been gone.

"We decided to work as hard as you if we were going to live here. We agreed to all go on a trip. Jack, Franz, Ernest, and I went out with water, an axe, and some guns. We followed Turk, who led us the way you had taken."

She smiled as she told us more of her adventures with the other boys while we were at sea.

"We were startled by amazing birds everywhere and found some giant trees. As we looked at them, I had an idea. What if we could build a house in these giants? It seemed to be perfect. And with that, we went to the beach and looked for anything else left from the wreck. As we looked, we saw the dogs eating something in the rocks…"

"Crabs!" said Jack.

"Yes," said my wife, "and the dogs also led us to the turtle eggs that we're now eating."

"Well," I said, "you'll have to show me your tree palace, and we can decide if we can live there like birds!"

"It might just work," she answered. "And it would save us from the jackals. If we could build a staircase and a nice floor, we would be safe at night."

"Alright," I answered, "let's look tomorrow and see if it will work." And with that, we all went to bed and slept deeply.

The next morning, my wife and I woke and

discussed our plan. We agreed that if I could build a bridge across our river and could find a safe place far up in the rocks to stow dangerous things such as gunpowder away from our house, we might just make it all work.

We woke the children and set about to making our bridge. Ernest, Fritz, and I set sail again for our wrecked ship to take boards from it. Soon, we saw some birds feeding on a giant fish on an island and drew close to watch.

"Fritz," yelled Ernest, once we had gotten close, "it's the shark you shot. You must have hit him in the head!"

It was true. As we drew close we saw what a monster the shark had been, with rows of shining, terrible teeth. We jumped onto the island and cut off the shark's fin as a prize and found the island there full of boards and beams from the wreck, perfect for our bridge back near our beach. We put these on our boat and headed back.

When we reached our beach, we were met by the boys and my wife, who showed us bundles of crawfish that Jack and Franz had found. As we cooked these, we began to plan our bridge.

My wife had created a bag for the donkey to carry gear over the river, and I built a pulley from a tree to lower wooden beams from one shore to the other. Soon, we had set down all the beams needed to make a flat bridge, and the children danced across the river with joy. By the time this work was done, we were exhausted and made our way to bed, happy with our progress.

The next morning, I told everyone, "Even though we are moving to the trees, we are not safe and we still need to be careful. Who knows what danger lies ahead?"

With this warning, we began to move all we had in the world to the site of our new home. The children ran to gather the chickens, ducks, and geese, and Franz rode the donkey across the bridge. The other boys helped lead the animals across the river and soon we were all on the other side. As we came upon our future home, we knew it would make a wonderful place to live.

Soon enough, the boys were all helping. Ernest found stones to build a fireplace, while Franz discovered that the trees where we were going to build our home were filled with wild figs. He fed these to the baby monkey, named Knips by the boys. We also hunted some birds and managed to capture a live flamingo, which we decided to keep and add to our other birds.

We then searched the trees to pick one we thought was best. We set out to find bamboo to build platforms because it would be strong and would hold up well in the rain. Searching in a nearby marsh we were lucky enough to find plenty for our use. We decided that we would live thirty feet up the tree, so I built a ladder to take us to our first platform.

Once the ladder was done, we hauled up all that we could and set about making makeshift hammocks around the tree branches for sleeping in the next night. We were very tired by all of our work, so we ate dinner and slept by the fire at the foot of our new home.

The next morning, we began to get our home ready by cutting branches out of the way, building platforms, and making walls from planks and sails. Soon enough, we had a place of our own and had our first meal among the trees, laughing and happy with Knips the monkey. When we pulled up our ladder that night we felt safe and secure. We were together in our new home, high among the branches.

CHAPTER 5

A Strange Meal

ᔑ

The next morning we woke and the boys jumped up, excited about what our next adventure might be.

"What shall we do now, Father?" they asked.

"Rest," I answered. "It is Sunday."

With that, we all decided to simply have a day of fun and relaxation. After breakfast I built bows and arrows for the boys, even a little set for Franz. The boys quickly learned how to use them. No sooner did they finish practicing than I heard the sounds of two birds falling from the branches, shot by Ernest. He was thrilled to have caught our dinner.

"Well," said Ernest, "with the bridge in place, it's feeling like a home, isn't it?"

"Yes," answered Jack, "but what shall we call all of these places?"

"We need to name them ourselves," suggested Fritz, "to make them our own."

Fritz suggested calling our landing spot Safety Bay. We all liked this name and carried on with our game.

After that, we decided to call the spot where we built our first camp on the island Tentholm. We named our island Shark Island, and our swamp Flamingo Marsh. We agreed to call our new tree house Falconhurst and the land in which we lived New Switzerland.

The next day, I suggested we head to Tentholm by a different route so we could explore more. We all trekked back in a line, looking quite a sight with our monkey riding our dog. Suddenly, I heard Ernest shout out happily, and we all ran ahead.

"Look," he shouted, "Potatoes! Lots and lots of potatoes!"

Sure enough, he had discovered an entire field of potatoes, which meant we would never starve. We all got down and started to dig up our new find. Our funny little monkey followed our lead. Loaded down, we continued on our new route. We made so many discoveries as we walked. Palms, flowers, cactus, jasmine, vanilla, peas, and pineapples all lay in our path. I was happy to recognize some karata plants, which were perfect for making rope and string. I also showed my wife and sons how to use the pit of the plant to make fire by hitting the pit with a rock. Sure enough, it sparked, and they were thrilled to learn how to do it.

Jack tried to pick some Indian figs. He found

the prickles hard work but finally managed to pierce one with a stick. We broke it open to get to the fruit inside and ate it happily for a snack. Soon, they were asking me questions about every plant that we passed until finally I told them to stop.

"Boys," I admitted, "the truth is that I don't actually know everything about all these plants and animals, but together we will learn much more about our island."

Finally, we were at Tentholm. We began to collect the rest of our important things and set about catching the ducks and geese, which Ernest baited with cheese. Once back at our new tree home, we feasted on potatoes, butter, and cow's milk. With Falconhurst stocked, we turned in for the night.

The next day, Ernest and I decided to look on the beach for driftwood. A driftwood sled would come in handy for carrying supplies back and forth between the two places.

We took our donkey, loaded the wood onto it, and went back to camp to make our sled. When we arrived, the other boys were catching more birds. My wife had suggested that the boys build traps to capture, but not kill, the birds. She explained that we could be here for a while so we needed to make sure we planned our food for the future. As they worked on this idea, we built our sled. Everyone was busy and happy.

Franz, being youngest, wanted to help, too. He suggested that we should plant gunpowder in the ground. "That way we could grow something really more useful than vegetables." The boys all laughed at poor Franz, as I explained to him how gunpowder was made.

As soon as the sled was finished, Ernest and I set off back to Tentholm. Once there, we again gathered supplies. Just as we were about to leave with all we could fit onto the sled, we noticed the animals were nowhere in sight. Ernest searched for them as I went to cut more sugarcane. Returning, however, I found Ernest asleep.

"Ernest," I said, waking him, "if the animals have made their way off the beach by crossing the bridge, we may have lost them for good, and we will be very sorry for that!"

"But look, Father," he said, "I have pulled up one of the beams of the bridge and the animals can't cross until we put it back." I laughed at his idea and was sorry for scolding him. While I replaced the bridge beam and checked the loaded sled, Ernest decided to try fishing in the river with a branch for a pole, some string and one of the hooks Franz had found on the ship. He called me loudly almost right away, and I came running to see that he had caught himself a giant of a fish. As he lay in the grass trying to pull it from the river, I noticed that it was a salmon, almost fifteen pounds!

I hugged him with joy as we made our way

back to the sled. I was proud of my son and relieved to know that he could take on a lot of family responsibility.

On our way back to our tree house, we suddenly spotted a giant beast leaping through the woods! Ernest shot at it and knocked it down. As we ran to get a closer look at the animal, we saw that it was as big as a sheep, with a head like a mouse, a tiger's tail, and ears like a rabbit. We looked at it for a long time, amazed by its appearance until suddenly I clapped my hands.

"It must be a kangaroo! And you are the first to have found one in New Switzerland!"

We somehow got our new prize onto our overloaded sled and made our way to Falconhurst to show the other boys what we had found. We came back to discover them dressed in clothes they had found from the wreck, each looking like a little pirate. Fritz alone seemed upset that his little brother Ernest had had such luck hunting. I took Fritz aside to tell him how important his work taking care of the family was to me, but he made me promise to take him along next time.

That night, the whole family and the dogs had a delicious and strange meal that I never would have imagined in our home back in Switzerland: potatoes, salmon, and kangaroo.

CHAPTER 6

A Tow to Shore

〜

I woke the next day and began to tan the kangaroo hide, as I thought it might come in handy. When taking a short break, I looked for Ernest and Jack. My wife thought they might have taken Turk along for company when digging up more potatoes or getting other supplies. It worried me that they were on their own, but there wasn't much I could do about it. I left my wife with little Franz while Fritz and I set off for our boat. As we crossed the bridge, Ernest and Jack sprang out from the bushes, taking us by surprise. We fell together laughing, and they begged us to take them to the ship. Instead, I sent them back with a message to their mother that Fritz and I would stay overnight on the wreck to get more done. They sulked away to tell their mother the news.

We took our little boat out on the current and talked together of building another boat to carry heavy items. Once at the wreck, we found the wood we would need for more building, the barrels and beams to make our larger boat, and some empty chests that would be perfect for storage. Before ending the day, we made our new boat and launched it as we had the last. After all of that heavy work, hunger overtook us. We made a great feast from the ship's supplies and slept on mattresses, feeling like kings.

The next morning, we took all the chests we could carry, loaded our larger boat with furniture and window frames, more cooking supplies, and even a chest of gold. We also discovered some baby fruit trees still alive that we were thrilled to be able to plant. These were apples, pears, chestnuts, oranges, almonds, peaches, plums, and cherries.

We located tools, paint, wheels, spades and shovels, sacks of wheat and dried peas, and the parts to make a mill. It seemed unbelievable that we had found so much but we understood that it was all supposed to go to start a new colony before our wreck. Our greatest find by far were mattresses that we knew would make our family overjoyed. We counted ourselves lucky indeed!

Fritz, remembering his shark, grabbed a ship's harpoon that he got ready, just in case. And then, both boats loaded, we were ready to set off. As we did, I heard Fritz call me from behind the sail.

"Father!" he called out. "Steer this way, quickly!" I did as he asked and suddenly felt the boat being pulled toward the shore. I looked around the sail to find an amazing sight.

Fritz had managed to hook his harpoon on the shell of a sea turtle, and it was pulling us to shore with great speed. As the turtle reached the shore, it pulled itself up on the beach and we had a fine landing. The turtle was very tired after pulling us and was easy to catch and pull up into one of our tubs.

As we landed, our family ran toward us to see all that we had brought back, including our mighty turtle. The boys ran off to get the sled so we could transport back as much as possible could before nightfall.

We managed to get the turtle onto the sled and then, carrying some of our fruit trees, we made our way home, talking about our adventures.

"I would like you to look at some roots I found," said Ernest, "I think they might be useful."

In fact, Ernest had found a root could be made into flour. It would be lovely to have bread for the first time since we landed.

We all made our way back to camp and, once we had arrived, unloaded the treasures we had found. My wife gave us some sugarcane juice she had made that was delicious to drink, and we all had some with our dinner. That night, we slept warmly in our treetop palace, on our wonderful new beds.

I woke early to our happy home and after working for a while I came back to find everyone still asleep. They woke surprised at how late it was. We all laughed and blamed it on the amazing mattresses.

After breakfast, Fritz and I readied ourselves to head back to the wreck again. This time, Jack looked simply too sad, so I took him with us. He was thrilled to come on the trip and help us to collect a few things to take with us. Jack was free to explore the wreck and, sure enough, he came out with a great find: a wheelbarrow! We made our way back to shore to see a strange sight: a troop on the beach that looked like stooped men in black jackets and white pants.

"Maybe they're pygmies!" said Jack.

"No, Jack," I laughed, "they're penguins!"

When we landed on shore, Jack ran after them. While most got away, he managed to tackle about six of them, which we decided to take back with us. We made our way home to find Ernest and my wife eager for our return.

Once settled in, we all settled down to grinding the root Ernest had found into flour for bread. We grated it onto a sail and then squeezed the juice out of what we had ground until we had wet flour. When done, we stored it and planned to make bread the next day. In the morning, we added water and salt to the flour and put the mixture on a plate heated by the fire, where it baked as if in an oven. When done, we were only too happy to eat the delicious treat.

That night, we ate penguin (which was fishy and tough) and potatoes. The other penguins seemed to have become friendly with the chickens. We set them free and they wandered happily with the flock, perfectly tame. We all stood in wonder, looking at the strange herd of animals that was now a part of our family.

CHAPTER 7

Sports Day

Soon after, I convinced my wife to let me take all the boys but Franz to the wreck once again, this time to try and fix up the little sailboat that I had seen in pieces on the deck.

She agreed, as long as I promised to have them back and not spend a night on the wreck. It was settled and we sailed out. While the boys searched for new things, I tried to decide how to get the boat out. We didn't quite get the job done and returned to find my wife and Franz on the beach.

"Until we have gotten everything we need from the ship, I have decided we should live at Tentholm. Trekking back and forth like this is wasting too much time," she said proudly.

It was a good decision and we spent the next days going from the beach to the ship, building the sailboat, and coming home to our first beach tent, happy and tired. Finally, after days, we had built the sailing boat on the deck of our wreck. But now we couldn't get it over the high deck railings of the ship. The only solution was to somehow blow out one of the railings of the deck to allow us to push the boat into the water.

I found a big cannon shell, filled it with gun-powder, and set a long fuse. With the fuse lit, I hurried the boys onto our little boat, rowed our way to the beach where my wife was waiting, and just as we landed, there was a giant bang on board the ship with much smoke.

I loaded the boys back onto the little boat, and once again we made our way back out to sea and to the ship. There, we found our wreck even more wrecked! Our "bomb" had worked! The side of the ship closest to shore was blown away. We now could put rollers underneath the sailboat on the deck of the ship and let it slide right into the water. The boys and I then spent our time fitting the sailboat with two small brass guns, much like cannons.

Finally, we set back for the beach with our old boat and our new sailboat, and as we got closer, I let the boys fire one of the brass guns with a bang. My wife and Franz ran out from our tent on land. We could see them jumping with excitement as they saw us. When we landed, we all laughed and hugged, very proud of ourselves, and my wife admired our beautiful sailing vessel.

"Now," she said, "you have to see what Franz

and I have done to make things better here on land!"

They took us on a tour of a garden they had made. "We've planted potatoes, sugar cane, fruit trees, melons, peas and other vegetables," my wife explained. "We've put the seeds where they will grow best." I told her she had done a great thing and as it began to get dark, we headed back to the tent to relax, feeling very tired.

The next day, I taught the boys how to use a lasso to catch a wild animal. We spent the morning practicing, and it was Fritz who became the real master of it. Later, we decided to go back to our Calabash Wood (as we had named it) to make more bowls and spoons and other things we might need. We loaded our sled with guns and powder and, with our donkey pulling it, called to our dogs to follow us. Our little monkey, Knips, would not be left behind, so we carried him along with us as our mascot. When we got to the coconut stand, Ernest stood underneath a tree.

"I wish I could have a coconut," he said. As soon as the words left his mouth, a coconut landed right beside him, making him jump. It seemed like magic until another and another fell. Sure enough, we knew something was throwing the coconuts at him.

We looked up to see that there was something in the tree. It quickly dropped down and started chasing Jack as the dogs barked and chased both of them. "It's a coconut crab!" I laughed. It chased Jack around until we finally caught it.

It was difficult making our way through the bush toward the gourds we needed. We cut our way along with some trouble until we reached the woods, where we set to work carving our dishes, bowls, and plates from the gourds and filling the finished items with sand to help them dry.

We made a fire, cooked our coconut crab, and gave our little monkey some coconut milk. After dinner, Ernest went for a walk through the woods but quickly came back shouting, "A wild boar! Come quick!"

We chased the boar through the woods madly with the dogs until we had it in a clearing. We were all excited until we saw that in fact it was one of our own pigs that had followed us. We all fell down laughing again. After that, we continued on our walk until Jack, who was ahead of us, cried out once again in surprise.

"A crocodile!" he yelled. "Come see!"

We again ran, and this time found a giant iguana, which we captured. We tied it up so it was safe to carry and took it back to camp, over my shoulder. On the way home, the boys gathered acorns and a new type of fruit, which we first gave to the monkey to test. He ate it happily, so we all tried it and were thrilled to find that it was a guava. We made our way back to Falconhurst and had an incredible dinner of iguana, potatoes, and roast acorns, with guava for dessert. We were getting used to these unusual meals.

CHAPTER 8

Explosion!

⤮

The next day, Fritz and I returned to Calabash Wood and decided to do some more exploring. We found a plant with a berry that I recognized as the kind that could be boiled to get out wax for making candles. We gathered the berries and continued to explore until we found a colony of parrots among the trees. Fritz climbed a tree to try and catch one. He was bitten on the hand for his trouble, but did manage to grab a parrot and put it in his pocket. When he came down, he showed me his pretty green bird. He decided to try to teach it how to talk.

Making our way back, we stumbled on some gummy syrup coming from a tree. Touching it, we found that it was quite stretchy.

"Look, Father, could it be rubber?" asked Fritz.

"Let me see," I answered. "You're right, it is! This will be perfect for making boots and shoes!"

We made our way back to Falconhurst and told everyone about our adventures. Everyone was so excited about the idea of making candles that we thought we would all try our hand at it right away.

We boiled our berries over the fire, scooped out the wax, and put it into another pot. Then, we took strings and dipped them into the pot of hot wax. Sure enough, as we let them dry and continued to dip them until they were thick, we found we had made candles. That night, for the first time, we had light at night at Falconhurst. It was an amazing thing.

The next morning, we tried to make butter from cream that we had skimmed off the top of the cow's milk. We put it in a gourd and rolled it back and forth for half an hour in a sail. And it worked! We were thrilled to open the gourd to find perfect butter inside. Things we used to take for granted at home suddenly filled us with great joy.

We then started a long project of making Tentholm a safe place to go in case of emergency. We wanted to get it all ready just in case we needed it. I planted a prickly hedge to block out animals and mounted two guns at its entrance. We were ready for attack by man or animal.

We passed our days on the island in projects, exploring, and hunting, and every Sunday I taught the boys to swim and climb. As a result, they became very strong over time, but soon enough their clothes were in tatters from all of their activities. The boys needed shoes, so my next task was to try making them from the rubber we had found. I did this by filling a pair of socks with sand. Around these sock forms, I laid clay, making a mold that hardened. On this clay mold, I painted rubber, layer after layer, until I had built up a pair of rubber boots. I was thrilled with my new boots, but I worried about what we would use for clothing, especially when the winter started.

I wondered if there were any clothes still on the wreck and decided that the older boys and I should return to the wreck one last time. We would take all the supplies that were left and would destroy the wreck once and for all. After filling our boats with everything we could find, we rigged the ship to blow up and headed to shore to watch our fireworks. As we made dinner and watched, a giant pillar of fire rose up with a massive roar. Our ship—our main connection to old Switzerland, our former home—was no more.

CHAPTER 9

A Growing Family

ᴄᴏ

We headed back to Cape Disappointment, which we named after we could not find any of our shipmates there. For this trip, I decided to take the whole family. We stopped and gathered more of the waxberries and found a nice spot to rest in a clearing between the sugarcane and bamboo.

"Why not live here?" asked Jack.

"It is lovely," I said, "but imagine a tiger coming out of the woods and trapping us here."

We all looked into the woods and shared the

worry. Still, we had to do our work. As it grew dark, our donkey ran off and the dogs chased it, but when the dogs came back the donkey was not with them. We made a big fire, and I told the boys to sleep beside their weapons as we lay down nervously in the clearing.

The next morning, I left the bigger boys to protect their mother and told Jack he could come with me to try and find our poor donkey. He was proud to be asked. After trudging for hours following the donkey's hoof prints, we saw that they joined with many others. Cutting our way through the forest, we came upon an amazing sight. Our donkey had joined a herd that stood by the river—a herd of giant buffalo! Before we could stop them, our dogs ran out into the herd and attacked a calf. The herd began to bellow and with a rush attacked us all at once, their horns flashing. We ran to back toward the forest but the leader of the herd, a giant, was already on top of us before we could reach it. At the last minute, I pulled my pistol and shot him dead. This stopped the herd, and they turned tail to run.

Still, our dogs were trying to take down the calf. Jack acted quickly, calling off the dogs, and swinging his lasso as the calf fell. All at once, he had the calf by the feet, and I tied the other end of the rope to a tree. We now had ourselves a live buffalo calf to try and tame. The children named the calf Storm.

We took what we could from the fallen buffalo, made a leash for our calf out of Jack's lasso, and walked him home. As we headed out, the dogs ran ahead. Suddenly, a pack of jackals appeared, drawn by the dead buffalo. They all fell into a fight with our dogs. The dogs won this fight and chased away the pack. We did, however, manage to rescue one small jackal to take back with us.

Getting back to our camp, we found our family excited at our new pets. Jack jumped about telling the story of what had happened, bragging a little. I let him tell his stories. He had done well.

The family had been busy, too, while we were gone. They had collected some wood that had washed up from the wrecked ship, and had gone hunting. Fritz had found a young eagle by Cape Disappointment. We decided to try and raise it as a hunting bird.

As we headed back to the camp, the boys went for another walk and began calling to me suddenly. I ran into the woods, thinking they were in danger, only to find them with our sow, lying on her side, surrounded by piglets. Our family continued to grow!

CHAPTER 10

A Tree with Stairs

〜

My wife asked if I could invent a way to reach our tree house without having to climb the ladder. It was a good challenge, and the boys and I got to work on it. We thought we might carve steps inside the trunk if it was hollow, which we hoped it was. The boys looked in a hole in the tree trunk and found it hollow—but full of bees that came swarming out to attack them.

We smoked the bees out by stopping up the hole with a hollowed piece of bamboo. I lifted up some hot coals from the fire and blew smoke from them through the bamboo until the bees were sleepy. We then quickly cut another hole in the trunk, and the bees flew out to get away from the smoke and were gone. We took what we could of their honey and wax, then carved the space where they had come out wider and wider until it was the size of a full door.

Later, we attached a door from the ship to the hole in our tree with hinges we had taken from the ship. It was perfect.

We spent several days hollowing out more of the tree to make our stairs and built wooden steps leading around the inside of the trunk. Soon,

we had a staircase, complete with a railing for holding.

During our weeks of this work, our animals all had babies of their own. We trained our buffalo to till our fields. We tamed our jackal so that we could raise it with our puppies. I even trained our eagle and got Knips to ride the buffalo.

One morning, while we were working, we heard a very loud roaring. We had no idea what it could be. A lion? A gorilla? A tiger? We were all worried and climbed up to our house where we loaded the guns. Fritz and I decided it was best to go into the woods to find what it was, or we all would always be afraid. We snuck through the brush, fearing some monster beyond our understanding. As we grew nearer, the sound grew more intense. We cringed, cocked our guns, and pulled back the branches, to find ourselves staring at a sight that had us laughing wildly.

The sound was from our donkey, which had come home with a new friend—a wild donkey! We led them back to our camp by offering tidbits of food. It took us days to tame the wild one. I had to jump on its back and ride it to tire it out and calm it down. At long last, it became calm and friendly.

One night we took Knips to the woods to fill our sacks with acorns. The little monkey ran up a tree and discovered the eggs of a grouse. We covered them and took them back to our house where my wife kept them warm, wrapped in blankets by the fire. In a few days, they hatched. My wife had been working with our birds and had raised more than forty chickens. The grouse chicks added more birds to our growing flock.

Ernest had been busy cutting long, thick grass for Franz to play swords with back at camp. Franz had the time of his life, dancing about and battling imaginary enemies. After examining his sword more closely, I noticed that it was a plant called flax. My wife was overjoyed.

"If you can make me a spindle I can spin this flax into yarn. We will all have new clothes! With that, we took our donkeys and buffalo and brought back all the flax we could.

We worked extra hard before winter came to make stables on the grounds, stack away hay, and build a dairy, kitchen, and dining hall under our one roof in our giant tree home. There was not much more time to get ready. We spent the next days storing potatoes, coconuts, acorns, sugarcane, and whatever other food we found as quickly as we could harvest them. Each day the sky grew darker and thunder rattled in the distance. Soon, cool showers turned to icy cold—and never-ending—winter rains.

The weather was fierce. Each day we had to take shelter in the trunk of our crowded tree house. The smell of the animals was not pleasing, and the smoke from our fire made us cough. My wife brushed some of the rubber we had found on to our hooded shirts to make them waterproof. Soon she had made us full waterproof suits to wear.

The days were long and hard. We tried to pass the time as best we could. I wrote all that had happened in my journal, my wife sewed, Ernest made sketches of birds, and Fritz and Jack taught little Franz to read. The weeks rolled by. We were prisoners of the winter. It was a gloomy time for all.

CHAPTER 11

The Cozy Cave

∽

After weeks and weeks, the rains stopped, and
we were free again! We heard the birds sing and
felt the warm sunny air on our faces. Our seeds
were coming up. Spring was here, and there was
plenty to be done. We were full of joy.

We visited Tentholm to find it blown to pieces
by the storms. Everything was soaked. Our old
boat was ruined, and we knew that we had to do
better next year. We found our way to the cliff face
beside the beach and decided to begin to dig there
a cave for storage. We drew a door in chalk and

hacked away at it for ten days, making slow progress. Suddenly, with a loud thud, Jack fell heavily and called to me.

"Father, my chisel has gone through!"

We laughed at first but then saw that it was true. I reached through the hole. There was only a small layer of rock between a cave and us! We all chipped away with real energy and joy and found that it was a great cave indeed. The whole family marched in, poking our way with a long stick. And then, by candlelight, we saw that all around the cave was crystal and shining. Everything sparkled and shimmered with all the colors of the rainbow. I ran my finger along the cave wall and then licked it. I was right. It was giant cave of salt! The floor was made of dry sand. It would be a fine new shelter.

As we walked back, we all talked of how Falconhurst should now be our summer home only. The cave was perfect for the winter once it was all fixed up. We decided on the spot to call our new home Rockburg.

We cut windows beside our door, in the thin wall of the cave front for light and air and divided our new home into rooms. We even built ourselves a chimney and a new stable within the giant space. One day, while building, we saw a light in the water nearby and saw swooping birds flying in to eat all they could. We ran out and stood to watch.

"What is it?" asked the boys.

"A school of herring!" I answered. The fish were in shallow water and were easy to scoop out by the hundreds, using only our hands. There was no time to waste. With the barrels we had, we started to catch, dry, salt, and store the herring for our next winter. Months later, even more fish came. These were giant sturgeon that swam their way along the shore.

"Quick," said Jack, "let's catch them!"

71

"Yes," I answered, "but how? These fish are much bigger than the herring."

Jack ran off laughing and came back with a bow and arrow and his fishing line. He tied the line to the arrow and fired into the fish. Sure enough, he hit one in the side and it almost pulled him into the river.

"Help, Father, or I'm going in!" he cried, and we both pulled and pulled until the great fish was on the shore.

Soon, all of us were spear fishing, catching bigger and bigger fish. Fritz even got one that was eight feet long, too big for us to get out of the water. We had to get our buffalo to come and pull it out. We used salt from our cave to cure these fish for winter, too.

It seemed like food was everywhere. Our gardens were blooming and coming to life. Corn was coming up, as were fields of barley, wheat, rye, and peas. While the boys and I had been adventuring, my wife had been planting everywhere. Now, we would all eat like kings and still store plenty of food for the coming winter.

As we were out one day, looking over our crops, we came upon white fluff all over the ground.

"Snow!" cried Franz.

"No, my boy," I said, "this is not snow. It's cotton!" And I was right. Soon, we were gathering it into bundles for spinning and making more clothes.

During this time, we started and finished many projects. It was a busy time, as we were set to build our own colony now. We found a perfect place to make a new farm with a grassy hill and shady trees along the river. We were determined to harvest all that we could from the land. This seemed a spot where we could plant cotton and other crops that we might need for clothing.

We set about right away to make a simple log

barn on the spot so that our animals could be happy and safe on the land, even if we were not there. We built a place in the barn for animal stalls and perches for our birds.

We found a hill nearby during this time and built a small cottage named Prospect Hill. It was a simple building of logs, but it would be a nice home for us to visit when we planted or cleared the crops on this land. During this time, we also made a bark canoe from a tree. Tired but content after this busy time building our new farm home, we made our way back to Falconhurst, and then to Tentholm.

Upon returning, we found that one of our cows had had a bull calf. I asked Franz if he would care to train it.

"Oh, yes, Father!" he said, "and I will call him Grumble because of the noise he makes!"

We all thought this was perfect and we set back to work on our cave. We made the floors flat and finished the rooms. We even made a carpet from the hair of some of our animals.

The next day was the first anniversary of our landing. We decided to call it Thanksgiving Day. I awoke that morning to a loud bang. Running out of the cave, I saw that the boys had fired the cannon to celebrate. They said they were sorry, but I could tell they were proud. We decided to celebrate with a day of sports.

We started with archery, where Fritz was the champion, and then moved on to races. I sent Fritz, Ernest, and Jack to run from Tentholm to Falconhurst and bring me back a penknife I had left there. They took off like a shot and were soon out of sight. But not long afterward, something very strange happened.

Jack appeared speeding across the bridge. But he wasn't on foot. He was riding the buffalo, followed by our pair of donkeys.

"I saw that I wasn't going to win," he told us,

laughing, "so I thought I might as well come back in style!"

Ernest was first back with the knife and declared the winner. Next, it was the climbing test. In this race, Jack climbed like a mountain goat and outshone all his brothers. He was up a tree faster than they could begin.

Franz entertained us with a show. He came from the cave and announced, "Judges, I present to you something new and amazing. I, the bull tamer, will now show you amazing tricks!" Out came Grumble the bull on a leash, running, trotting, and jumping as we all clapped loudly. We finished the day with swimming. The boys were all very good, but Fritz again was the strongest.

When the contests were finished, my wife was ready with prizes that she had pulled from our ship's supplies. To Fritz, she gave the award for shooting and swimming. His prize was a new rifle and a hunting knife. Ernest, for winning the running, was given a gold watch. For climbing and riding, Jack got spurs and a riding whip, which made him very happy. Finally, Franz got stirrups made of rhino bone and a whip for training. Lastly, I gave my wife a beautiful box I had found on the old wreck and had saved for a surprise.

At the end of the day, the boys wanted to fire another cannon shot. We ended our day with a big bang that echoed along the beach. It had been a great day, and I was amazed how far we had come in just one year.

We smiled at the name and when I looked to see what it was, I was thrilled.

"Boys," I said, "this is ginseng. It is good for health and medicine. Well done!"

"The bad news," Fritz continued, "is that the farm has been almost ruined by the monkeys. They got into everything, and the animals and the cottage are a mess. We'll have to go back and take care of that."

Earlier we had caught pigeons by smearing the rubber onto the branches of trees and waiting for the birds to land and get stuck. I hoped this same plan might help with our monkey problem at the farm. We got to the farm and smeared the sticky stuff all around. We waited for the monkeys to arrive. Soon, they did arrive and were quickly stuck all over with the sticky sap. They even became stuck to bowls and other things we had left about for them. The dogs chased them, and the monkeys ran and scattered, never to return.

I thought again of our sticky monkeys when, one day soon after, Jack went off on his own to try and find a new thing to bring back to the family. Instead, he came back covered in slime and almost ready to cry. If he hadn't looked so bad, we would all have laughed.

"What happened?" I asked.

"I was trying to get some bamboo to build things with," he answered, "but I got stuck and fell in the marsh. Turk saved me by pulling me out!"

We all felt lucky to have such a pet and Jack's bamboo was exactly what I needed for my latest idea. I planned to make a weaving loom for my wife and this was what I wanted. When it was ready, she was overjoyed to have it and set it to use right away to weave our spun cotton thread into fabric.

I used the rest of the bamboo to build a pipe from the river going up to the cave and created suction until water ran up the pipe. It would be good during the winter to have running water. Winter would be fast approaching again. Soon, the rains would be back. It was time to harvest.

CHAPTER 13

The Long Winter

W e spent many days gathering roots, grains, fruits, and acorns. We filled as many of the rooms as we could with what we had. It started to become gloomy and cloudy again. Thunder and lightning were everywhere. The winter was not far off. We needed to be ready for twelve weeks of cold rain.

We spent our time in the cave making it warm and cozy. We used a large bamboo pole to hang a candle up high so we had light. We set up a library, putting our books on shelves and decorating the walls with maps and charts from the wreck. Jack and his mother made a living room and a kitchen and Fritz and I built a workshop. Our cave was endless. We were ready for winter.

My wife and I decided to use the winter months to school the boys. It was a good opportunity for our boys to learn a language other than our native German, so we all studied French from books saved from the wreck.

"I'm going to learn Spanish!" announced Jack.

"I just love how important people sound when they speak it!" The boys also tried to learn English and Dutch with their mother. Soon we had all learned a few words and phrases of both languages.

We also passed the time by opening up all the chests from the wreck and going through them for treasure. We found chairs and clocks, a music box, and many other things. In this way, we spent the long winter, but this time our home didn't feel like prison.

As the season closed, the weather became even wilder. Storms blew and lightening flashed. The wind was like a hurricane. And then, suddenly, it was over.

We went walking on the first dry day and saw something through our telescope on the far end of the beach. It looked like an overturned boat, and we decided to find out more. We were all happy to be back to exploring. Heading toward it, we noticed it was not a boat but a huge, stranded whale that had washed up and died. The storm had truly been a strong one. But the destructive storm had also washed up lovely coral and shells everywhere, which the boys collected. We walked back home to get tools to cut blubber from the whale. The oil would come in handy. Fritz and Jack climbed the whale to begin the work. As we cut into the whale, the air was filled with birds. The birds snatched at the whale and bothered us to no end. Once we had finally stripped the whale of fat and meat, we cut further into the whale to get bones to use as oil lanterns. We left the rest for the birds and loaded our boat with all that we could carry. We decided to call the place of our latest adventure Whale Beach. We got home, stinking and tired, and each had a bath, thanks to our bamboo water pipeline. We put on clean clothes and ate supper and were all happy to be done with our whale.

The next morning, I showed the boys how to get the oil from the blubber. It was a day of bad smells and an unhappy family. We all knew we needed the oil for lamps and other things, but the work was not what any of us wanted. We all decided that when the bones of the whale were picked clean by the birds, we should set up a camp there. That way, if we had messy work like this, we could keep it away from our home.

I then set about building a small rowing machine for our boat, which simply turned a cog that set the oars to row. Everyone was pleased and the next day, we decided to take the boat to Cape Disappointment and check on our animals. As we came close, we saw that they were afraid of us. We had been gone too long in our winter cave. The goats would not be milked and had to be lassoed to get the job done. We had to catch all of the chickens and birds all over

CHAPTER 14

Farewell to a Friend

∽

"Why don't we build a basket chair for Mother to ride in?" asked Fritz.

"Yes," said Ernest. "We can make it and then put it on the bull and the buffalo!"

Soon enough, the boys had hung a large basket between Storm and Grumble, and Fritz and Jack hopped up onto one animal each. Then Ernest got in the basket to test it out. They walked along slowly and it seemed to work wonderfully.

"It's great and smooth," said Ernest. "Fritz, go

faster!" Soon, the animals were racing along and Ernest was being bounced all over as his brothers laughed and laughed.

But our fun was to be short lived.

That day, as we were sitting on the porch of the cave, Fritz suddenly yelled, looking up the road.

"I can see something strange and terrible! It rises up and then goes flat like a cable. It slinks on huge coils. And it's coming for the bridge!"

I jumped up and looked through my telescope.

"It is as I feared," I cried. "It's a giant snake of some kind. And it's coming this way!"

"Let's attack it!" yelled Fritz.

"If we do, it will only come after us here in our home," I answered. "We must find a way to fight it away from here. Go and get the guns, and we'll all hide and watch it."

I watched the serpent come closer and sure enough it crossed the bridge, lifting up its massive head almost twenty feet in the air. It was out hunting prey. We hid as it crossed the bridge and got ready for it, our guns loaded and our hearts thumping.

As it came closer, it stopped, as if it had smelled us. It lifted itself up, moving its head from side to side. The boys couldn't resist and opened fire. Even my wife shot at the beast. But the shots had no effect, and it simply glided by our cave and into the marsh. We were free for the moment but we were all very worried.

"Boys," I said, "that was a boa constrictor. And I believe it is more than thirty feet long."

I told the family that no one was allowed to leave the house until we had killed the monster. We knew it was nearby, as we could hear our ducks and geese reacting in fear near the reeds.

Suddenly, they all flew away and didn't stop until they reached Shark Island. Until we could draw the snake into an open space away from our home, we were all trapped. Finally, we were saved by an unexpected hero: our donkey.

As we could not leave the cave to feed the animals, I shooed them out across the bridge to go back to their feeding place. But the donkey was too excited to be on the loose and it ran to the marsh. Suddenly, the boa reared up, its tongue flicking, jaws wide, and lunged on the poor animal. It was all over quickly.

"Father," cried the boys, "shoot the snake now!"

"Not yet," I told them. "Our best chance now is to wait until the snake has eaten its prey and then take it."

We all thought about our own lives and the giant snake so near by. My wife and Franz could not watch and went inside. Soon the snake lay almost asleep by the side of the river, bloated. Now was our chance to attack.

We stepped quietly, sneaking up with our guns drawn. The snake lay still, its tail twitching, its eyes fiery. We were all scared and excited. All at once, we fired on the monster's head and its eyes went dead. The whole family stood over it, amazed.

"Let's stuff it!" said Fritz. "We can put it in our museum!"

"Could we eat it?" asked Ernest.

"Of course not," said my wife. "Snakes are poisonous!"

"Not true," I answered. "In fact, people eat rattlesnakes and other snakes after they throw away the fangs. You can even make soup from them. But, Ernest," I asked, "can you first think of some words to say for the poor donkey, who gave his life for us?"

"Let me think," said Ernest, and we all waited.

"I have it," he said at last. "But you can't laugh."

"Of course not," I answered.

And so he began:

Beneath this stone poor Grizzle's bones are laid
A faithful friend he was and loved by all.
In the end, our call, he disobeyed,
And that is how he came to fall.
A serpent, springing from the grass,
Swallowed him before our eyes.
And even though he had to pass,
We're grateful that he saved the lives
Of all the people on this shore
Father, mother, and children four!

We all cheered his poem and I wrote it down on a flat stone, where we would later bury our hero.

After dinner, we dragged the snake away, and

then we skinned, stuffed, and sewed it up so the boys could study it. We set it in the museum with its jaws wide, curled around a pole, making it as scary as we could. We even made a tongue and a pair of eyes out of shiny beach stones to make it more frightful.

CHAPTER 15

The Biggest Danger Yet

᧒

After such a terrifying experience, none of us could quite relax. The only way to be sure we were safe was to scour the island for further dangers. I got the boys and we went out to explore once again. We would be gone for weeks, I explained to them as I planned for us to cross the island and discover all of the dangers it might hold. Until we knew, we could never rest easy and there might be worse than our fierce snake out there. We packed and got ready to travel.

One day, during our travels, I took Franz with

me to test his hunting skills, while the other boys rested. As we walked through a marsh, he came upon what he thought was a pig. He shot at it and when we got to it we found it was not. It was a capybara with bristles and yellow hair. We took it with us back to our camp and Franz showed off his trophy.

Everyone else returned with their own treasures. There were birds for dinner and Fritz had returned with some strange apples that we first let Knips try. Knips seemed to like them, so we gave them a bite. They were cinnamon apples and a real treat. We had found no serpents and were beginning to feel more at ease. We all slept well.

The next day, we

came upon some wild boar, which we caught and killed and made into hams that we smoked over some days. Later, we continued our search for serpents at Prospect Hill, only to find apes had been there, too. The place was a mess. We could not deal with it then as we had to keep up our search.

We carried on until we got to the end of the coast and stopped there. We pitched a tent again, and the next day the boys and I set out to explore this new land. As we walked, Knips suddenly ran off yelping. We looked to see what had upset him and thought we saw horsemen coming toward us. As they got closer, we saw that they were ostriches! As they passed, we discovered a nest full of their eggs. Each was as big as a baby's head, so we could only carry two away. We tied them in a handkerchief on a stick and carried them like a basket. From there, we made our way to the nearby water hole and looked at the tracks. There were all kinds of animal marks here, but no serpent. As we headed back to camp, we heard the dogs bark and saw Ernest running toward us at full speed.

"Father," he cried, "bears! There are bears chasing me!"

As the massive animals came out of the clearing, they chased at us on their back legs, rearing up to fight. We shot as quickly as we could and one fell to the ground. We hit the second just as it was rising up to strike Fritz.

"Thank heavens!" I shouted. "This was our biggest danger yet. We didn't find any serpents, but these bears would be just as deadly. We've done well today."

And with that, we set about getting ourselves some bearskin rugs. These we took back on our animals to camp. The next day, we set out for the spot where the bears had attacked and cut meat off the bears we had killed for our dinner that night. We smoked the rest of the meat on the spot to save for a later day. While we were there, we found plants that I knew were pepper. We soaked and dried them and made ourselves both black and white pepper.

During this time, I let Jack, Fritz, and Franz go out on their own adventure. Ernest and I stayed back to finish our work. The boys each took to their animals and were off like a shot. I wanted them to be brave and to learn how to take care of themselves. While they were gone, Ernest and I found that the bears' cave was lined with a kind of stone that could be seen through when split into thin pieces. I knew then that I could make windowpanes of it. My wife would be thrilled with this discovery.

As night came, we heard the sound of hooves coming. We knew our party of adventurers would be coming back. We saw them jump from their saddles and the boys all came rushing up to the camp. They were excited, and Fritz's bag looked lumpy and strange.

"Hurray for the chase, Father!" said Jack, "We've had such a good time!"

"Yes," said Franz, "we've found an antelope and rabbits and we even found a cuckoo that showed us where to find honey!"

"Well done!" I told them happily. "Most importantly, you are all back safe. Now, tell me the whole story."

And that is what they did.

CHAPTER 16

How to Ride an Ostrich

చా

"We had a great ride, galloping the whole way in the sun," Fritz told us. "And then, coming over a hill, we saw the antelope. We were going to hunt them, but then we thought we should try and drive them as a herd!"

"We rode down the hill yelling and shouting," continued Jack, "and, drove them along with the dogs."

"Great work, boys!" I said, "You have done an important thing. But I have to warn you that the rabbits you have caught might be a problem. Now that you have them, you might find you want to be rid of them. Soon, there will be too many!"

"That is why we think we should put them on Shark Island, Father," answered Fritz.

"I caught them," said Jack, "and you should have seen Storm and Grumble and the dogs and I chasing them! It was amazing...."

"And then," he continued, excited, "we saw a cuckoo and followed it as it hopped away. Franz thought it must be an enchanted princess under a spell. Fritz told us it would lead us to honey, and he was right! Sure enough, it led us to a bees' nest. We must have scared them because the bees flew out and stung me all over! I jumped on Storm and ran off, but they followed me the whole way!"

Out of breath, Jack ran off to check on his rabbits.

The next day, we went to check on the ostriches we had found. Jack and Franz ran ahead and suddenly we were upon the giant birds. This time, we found a pair in the bush and were quick to try and catch them. Again, our lassos came in handy.

As Jack and Franz drove the ostriches out of the reeds, Fritz set loose his eagle, which confused one. As the ostrich faltered, Jack chased it down, bravely threw out his lasso, and tied it round its wings and body. It fell and we ran up to it, but it was kicking madly. Finally, I put a hood over its eyes to calm it down. We had ourselves an ostrich to try and tame.

"I'm going to make a saddle so I can ride him!" declared Jack.

At this, the boys started arguing about who was the owner of the bird.

"I think I should have him!" said Franz. Each of the other boys had a reason for wanting the ostrich for their own. Finally, I settled it by saying that it was Jack's bird to train. "And," I added, "if he can tame it and saddle it, he can keep it."

The boys agreed and Jack seemed up for the challenge.

We threw the ostrich over the back of Storm, and the boys headed out to take it back to our camp, where we would get ready to set back for our winter home to load in our supplies. The next morning, we made our way home with our new walking bird.

Soon, we came through our farmyard to find it in good shape. Our animals were healthy, and it made us want to see our home in Rockburg even more. Our chickens, pigs, and goats were all growing their families. We also came across the herd of antelopes that Fritz and Jack had driven down. We watched them browsing in the reeds and talked about how beautiful they were.

While we were at the farm, we fixed what we could and then set off for Rockburg the next morning. By then, we were all thrilled to be back, and we threw open the doors and windows and aired out our home. While Jack worked on taming the ostrich, I tried to hatch the eggs by wrapping them in cotton and heating them over the stove.

The next day, Fritz and I headed to Shark Island to start our rabbit colony and to transport a pair of antelope. Then it was time to turn our mind back to our house and stowing our goods.

Jack's ostrich was proving difficult to train and seemed weak and sad. Finally, we managed to feed it balls of flour mixed with butter. It seemed to perk up, stretching out his long neck for another mouthful. Soon, it was back to full strength and quite tame. We were amazed to watch it eat all kinds of grains and fruit, washing them down with small pebbles to digest its food. After a month of training, it would walk and gallop on command. But how could we saddle an ostrich? I made a kind of hood for it with straps to hold on to, and built a small saddle that strapped under it. When the bird was ready, we decided to call it Master Hurricane because of its speed.

When we finally tried riding the ostrich, we were amazed at how quickly it could run. We were able to go between Rockburg, which was quickly becoming our permanent place to live, and Falconhurst in no time at all. The bird was so fast that the boys once again argued about who owned it. I had to jump in and make a decision.

"The ostrich is Jack's," I said. "We may all use it if we need, but it is Jack's pet."

And so, Jack had his Master Hurricane to ride. Our journey had been successful and we all felt secure and safe settling in for the season.

CHAPTER 17

A New Boat

$\backsim\!\!\!\!\!\curvearrowright$

Soon enough, the black clouds of winter were ready once again to roll in. It was time for us to give up our adventures. That winter, however, even with all of our hobbies, we felt trapped by our cave house.

"Why don't we make a light kayak for the spring?" suggested Fritz.

It seemed like a good idea to keep us all busy, and we worked hard on building the boat during the long winter.

Finishing our work on the kayak after many

weeks, we noticed the weather changing, the world blooming, and the birds singing again. As the rains cleared, we dragged our beauty into the open air. It was lovely just to be outside. We left the kayak and sailed out all together in our old boat to check the health of our animals. We found our antelopes well. As we were leaving Shark Island, my wife began gathering seaweed to bring back in her bag.

"What is it for?" I asked her.

"It's a surprise," she answered with a twinkle in her eye and I was left to wonder.

One afternoon some weeks later, after the incident had passed my mind, she came out from Rockburg with a jar of clear jelly. We all gathered around and tasted it. It was sweet and delicious.

"What is it?" I asked.

"Do you remember that seaweed I found a while ago?" she answered.

"Yes, of course," I said.

"This is what it makes. I learned it once from a friend."

We all told her she was a genius, and the boys were thrilled with the treat. My wife was pleased with our happiness, and we all promised to collect more seaweed.

Knowing our antelopes were well, we next checked on our rabbits. We found the grass and weeds there chewed by many little teeth. We could not see them but we knew they had made a family.

The next day, the boys all went out on a grand hunt. They returned that night, galloping and excited, having caught all kinds of wild game and fowl. They were proud and I could see that they had become true hunters. They had also brought back cuttings from cinnamon and sweet-apple trees. Fritz was most proud of a bag of thistles he had collected.

"These are for making wool!" he told me, and he was right. The weed would be very useful.

At the same time, we gathered our corn and spent a lot of time fishing. We salted and pickled all that we had. With two barrels of salted herring saved from last year, we had everything we needed for winter.

Fritz wanted to try out the kayak now that all the food had been gathered. We launched him into the water and away he paddled. As his mother watched, worried to death, he showed that he could handle the boat. He headed out of Safety Bay and into sea. The other boys and I chased behind in our sailboat but could not keep up. He was soon gone from sight, which made us worry. Suddenly, we heard a shot ring out and saw a puff of smoke. We sailed as fast as we could to find out if Fritz was safe. He was, and he had harpooned himself a walrus!

"Fritz," I yelled, "congratulations on your

hunt. But you took us all by surprise by going so far out."

"I didn't mean to, Father," he answered, "but once I got in the current, I couldn't stop! And then I saw the walruses and got excited."

"Well," I told him, "you're lucky to have gotten away without being hurt. Walruses can be very dangerous. Now, what are we going to do with it? He must be fourteen feet long!"

"I'm glad you followed me father," he said, "At least with all of us, we should be able to get him onto the sailboat!"

While we talked, Fritz decided that the head of the walrus would look perfect on his kayak. I offered to tow his kayak along behind us, but Fritz wanted to head home the same way he had come. He wanted to show his mother that he was perfectly safe.

No sooner had we let him go than black clouds rolled in, bringing a giant storm. Fritz was out of our sight and we could not help him. The waves were so strong that we had to tie ourselves to the boat so that we would not be washed overboard. I was filled with worry for him and for ourselves.

My boys were brave and our boat held up. But I prayed that Fritz would somehow survive the wind and rain. Finally, as the weather began to clear, we made our way back to Discovery Bay.

As we got close enough to see the beach, we all laughed to see Fritz standing on shore. My wife was there, too, on her knees praying for us to return safely. The whole family was together again, home safely.

CHAPTER 18

Island Mail

⁓

The storm had wrecked many things and
everything was flooded. Our bridge had been
broken and our pipes were all burst. We had
much to do. After days of work, I could see the
boys were becoming bored. It was time for
another adventure.

Ernest decided to stay with his mother and
me, while the other boys got ready to go on a
journey to the farm. They left with Storm and
Grumble and the dogs. I noticed that Jack had left

with a cage full of pigeons, but I didn't really think much about it.

The next morning, while my wife and Ernest and I sat on the porch, we talked about how the boys might be doing on their adventure. Ernest told us just to wait and that we would know the next day. But just then, a pigeon flew into the coop and Ernest ran off. He came back with a small bit of paper in his hand.

"It's a letter from the pigeon post office!" he said.

We laughed at the wonderful surprise.

Ernest read the letter to us: "A hyena has killed a sheep and two lambs, but we have taken care of him. We are all fine. Love to all. Fritz."

Every night after that, we got a letter by pigeon telling us of the boys' adventures. After their hyena fight, Fritz took the kayak from the beach and paddled up the river, and the boys on the shore caught a pair of black swans. While they were there, they also saw an amazing animal come running out of the woods. By their description, I knew it was a tapir. Then they went back to the farm to collect all the cotton and rice they could.

Next, they headed up to Prospect Hill. They found it again taken over by monkeys who attacked them when they got there. After fighting off the monkeys, they spent a long and scary night alone.

"We are afraid," wrote Fritz, "because we heard a noise during the night that was so loud all the animals ran from it. It was a roar like an elephant and a lion, and the dogs were very scared. There are giant footprints everywhere. Come to us, Father. We are safe, but we are no match for this danger!"

After reading this last message by pigeon, I

jumped up and ran to my donkey. I told Ernest to come after me the next morning with his mother and supplies. I rode through the night by moonlight and got to the boys in the morning, out of breath. The boys were thrilled to see me, and we went to inspect the footprints. I thought they were from an elephant, but the more I looked, the more I thought it must be from an entire herd of elephants. They were nowhere to be seen, however, and we all spent a night telling tales around the fire, too excited to sleep.

The next morning, my wife and Ernest, along with the ostrich, got to camp and were happy to find us all safe. We decided to make a wall to keep out the elephants and then the boys explored. Fritz went upriver in his kayak and found banana and cocoa plants to take home to farm. When he came back, he told us what he had seen.

"I saw fifteen to twenty elephants feeding by the river and bathing in the marsh. And I saw jaguars on the banks! As I was getting close to the elephants, the water started to bubble around the kayak. I thought I had paddled into the middle of a spring. Just then, a hippo came up right beside my canoe and scared the life out of me! I turned and came rushing back to you!"

It was a wonderful story and it told us what kind of land was around us. Fritz handed his brother Jack a bag. Whatever was inside they kept a secret. Fritz begged me to be able to head back home by kayak and I told him he could.

We headed back and Jack carried the bag on the back of Master Hurricane. When we got back to Rockburg, he put his bag into the swamp. That night, we sat around and listened to Fritz's stories of his adventures on the kayak. Suddenly, we heard a loud and strange noise from the swamp. Jack jumped and ran at once as the boys all sprang to their feet. I turned to see Fritz laughing and waited to see what was to come.

Soon Jack came back with his wet bag. He opened it at our feet and out plopped a giant pair of frogs.

"This," said Jack, "is Grace. And this is Beauty."

With that we laughed and the frogs croaked away comically. It was a return worth remembering and we all turned in early, tired and spent.

The next day, we all set back to work, starting on a new project to put a flag post and a gun at Shark Island, in case of danger. Our plan was to fly a red flag for danger if we spotted it so the others could be warned and a white flag for calm. When the project was all finished, I let the boys celebrate by firing off the cannon with a loud shot that echoed round the island and had them laughing with joy.

CHAPTER 19

Not Alone

಄

Our lives went on like this happily and busily. Ten years passed in much the same way as we watched our sons grow and change into men.

We continued to take care of our land. We cleared the swamp and made a lake of it. We set swans there to rule the water. Our rabbits took over Shark Island, and our farm thrived.

Fritz was now twenty-four, strong and muscular and active. Ernest was two years younger and mild and calm. He liked to study and read. Jack, at twenty, was fast and flexible like Fritz.

Franz was seventeen and was witty and funny. They were all good men and kind to their mother and loved each other.

We still hoped that one day we would return to the company of other people. During our time in New Switzerland, the boys continued to have adventures and they often went off on their own to explore. One time, Fritz went off in his kayak and returned late that night with a heavy sack.

"I found many things in my travels, Father," he said. "I even came upon a bed of giant oysters in shallow water. I dived for them and pried them open to find these pearls."

We all gathered to look at his treasure.

"Well," I told him, "they are beauties. They have no value for us here, but some day they may."

Then, Fritz took me aside.

"Father," he said excitedly, "Something else incredible has happened. I also found an albatross, and it had a rag wrapped around his leg. When I caught it and unwrapped the rag, there were English words written on it! It said, "Save a poor Englishwoman from this smoking rock!"

"What did you do?" I asked, amazed.

"I took a rag of my own and wrote 'Do not worry. Help is near!' I tied this around the bird's leg and set it off. But now I wonder if it will ever find her."

"It could be that the note was quite old," I answered. "Don't tell the boys yet, as it may upset them. The writer could be long dead already."

Fritz said he felt that the writer was alive and that the smoke might be from a volcano. He wanted to find her. And so, after much discussion, I decided he could go.

"First," I explained, "we will set off together, and then I will let you go on your own."

Soon after, we set off with the boys, leaving behind only my wife and Franz, to see if I could set Fritz off on his own to find his fellow traveler. I allowed Fritz to put his kayak on board the boat and we set sail.

We traveled until we came to the Pearl Bay, which Fritz had named after his precious find and where he had found the note. We set up on the beach with a camp and a fire. The younger boys went exploring on the coast. Soon, Fritz and I heard shots coming from the shore. We both ran to see what was happening.

Jack had been attacked and had fired at a wild boar that had knocked him down and hurt him. We tended to him and soon he was asleep by the fire, healing. The next morning, Fritz headed off to look about and the boys and I found Jack's boar dead. It was a giant with great tusks, which could have easily killed him. All at once, a loud roar came from the jungle. Out from the trees came the biggest lion I have ever seen.

It prowled back and forth, pacing and watching us, growling. We were too frightened to move and had no weapons with us. As it grew more and more fierce, it suddenly ran forward at us. As it was in midair, a shot rang out. The lion fell to the ground and Fritz came out of the shadow. He had saved us all from the beast.

As we all gathered around the lion, a lioness suddenly came out of the jungle. After seeing her mate dead, she sprang at us too and Fritz had to shoot her as well. We were all sad to see the lioness killed but Fritz had saved us from sure death. I saw that he was now truly a man.

With this trial behind us, we loaded once more onto our boat. After a time, Fritz got ready to go on his own in the little kayak to have his adventure. As Fritz got ready to set out, I told the boys that he was simply looking for new finds. We named the spot Farewell Point as we watched him go. We set off again in our boat and Fritz went his own way, a man in search of his destiny. Only I knew his true purpose.

When we returned to our home, my wife was worried to see Fritz gone. I told her that he would return shortly and that he was simply exploring. Secretly, I had no idea when he would come back. We waited and worked, but after five days, I couldn't help worrying, too. I decided we should all go out in the boat to see if we could find him.

We sailed back toward the place where we had parted ways with Fritz when he set off in his kayak. As we came to Shark Island, we passed over a great whale that nearly took our poor boat down as it surfaced beneath us. We settled ourselves again and sailed on until we suddenly saw a dark figure in a kayak pass us by. He stood up and watched us and then steered his boat behind a rock.

All at once, I thought that this person must have taken poor Fritz. I raised our white flag and called out to the figure, but he was too far to hear my cries. Jack took up the call because his voice was far louder than my own.

"Look," he shouted, "come over here or we're going to come get you!"

With that, the kayak turned and started heading toward us. Suddenly, Ernest stood up and yelled.

"Hello, Fritz!" he said loudly.

"It's you!" Fritz answered with relief. "When I saw you, I didn't think you were my family. I thought you were pirates or natives, so I hid."

We described our adventure with the whale and he told us he had found another island where we could dock.

"Follow me!" he said.

With that, he turned around and headed out in his kayak. I let the boys steer and turned to tell my wife the truth about Fritz's mission. I told her about the note and that he might have found someone. She was filled with joy. But I

could tell she was also worried—and so was I—
about what we would find around the bend in
the shore.

As we landed on the shore of the island, Fritz
disappeared ahead of us. All of us were left to
wonder where he was. Suddenly, he came out,
holding a young woman by the hand.

CHAPTER 20

A New Islander

❦

"This," Fritz said, "is Jenny Montrose."

Our own boys leapt for joy and ran to embrace the first person other than our family they had seen in over more than thirteen years. They began to pepper the girl with questions and as they did, I saw my wife overjoyed to have a female friend to share our lives with.

Our new friend laughed and chatted with us, trying to find a way to say what had happened to her. We all talked at once, laughing and losing ourselves in the excitement.

After hours of sharing adventures, our new friend went off to bed. The boys asked Fritz how he had found Jenny. He began to tell the story of the albatross.

"It had a message attached to its leg. Only father knew. I sent a letter in return and then soon left in my kayak. I found many amazing things on my travels and would have stopped, but I was on a mission. When I reached a cove, I rested and made a fire and got a bird ready to eat. Out of the bushes then came a tiger with bright eyes that leaped out at me. Our pet

eagle lunged at him and surprised him long enough for me to get my gun. I only just got the pistol out in time and managed to knock him down with a shot. However, my eagle also lay dead.

"I got back in my boat after burying our friend and headed out to sea feeling sad and alone. But not for long. Soon, as I came around a bend, I saw a plume of smoke rising up. I raced with my kayak toward it, excited and breathless. I ran up the beach and toward the fire but there was no one there. Then I saw someone running. It was Jenny.

"She led me to the hut that she had made, with many items from her own shipwreck when she washed ashore three years ago. Like us, she had built many things and had learned to fish and hunt. She is the daughter of a British officer. She was on her way aboard a ship to meet her father when her ship was wrecked here. She was on a lifeboat that overturned and she was the only survivor. After gaining her strength, she would attach a message to any bird she could catch in hopes that she would be found. I heard her story and as I was in my kayak making a last trip to fish before heading to bring her home, I met up with you. I thought you were pirates and all was lost. Thank God it was my family!"

With that, everyone had many questions. We talked excitedly and as clearly as we could in our broken English until we were all tired. The next morning, the boys all greeted Jenny again with curiosity and excitement. We were thrilled to be able to invite Jenny to our home and to include her as part of our family. The day was beautiful and we stopped at Shark Island to launch a salute for Jenny as we introduced her to our humble home.

She reacted as if it were a palace. She had been alone so long and we had done so much work that it truly seemed a kingdom to her. Jack joked that all of our servants had run away just a few days ago. The boys outdid themselves setting out a dinner on all of our dishes and my wife found Jenny a dress to wear so that she could feel at home. We had a wonderful meal and then the boys took Jenny to show her all of our lands.

The next day, we started packing again for winter, which we knew was sure to come. As we worked, the boys treated Jenny like a queen and saddled a cow for her to ride sidesaddle. It wasn't long before she was just like one of us in our island kingdom. Her cheer made us happy.

Soon though, the winter came and we went back to Rockburg to wait for better days. But our time there was made happy with Jenny and the winter seemed short. She taught us to improve our English and we taught her to speak our language before the spring came. It was a wonderful time.

CHAPTER 21

Hello and Good-bye

ᐳ

With the passing of winter, we all came out again to the joy of spring. There was much to do for our expanded family and we took to the new days with great happiness.

One day, Fritz and Jack were out on Shark Island raising our flag when we heard a strange sound burst out. It was three shots from a gun. But had we really heard it? We all rushed to the beach to be sure. We were confused and happy and scared all at once. Was it friendly sailors or attacking pirates? All at once, the sailboat came back to shore from the island and Jack and Fritz jumped out to greet us.

"Did you hear that?" asked Fritz. "Father, what shall we do?"

I looked to the sky, only to see it was getting dark.

"There is nothing we can do tonight," I told them. "In the morning, we will set out to see what made the noise."

None of us slept that night, and in the morning a storm rolled in and made a mess of the shore. I knew that we would find nothing in that weather and so we waited again. The waiting was agony.

On the third day, we went out to Shark Island and fired off our cannons. There was no sound for a while, but then we heard a shot ring out again.

We came back to our beach, still worried that the ship might be full of pirates or enemies of

some kind. Fritz and I got into the sailboat with our guns and sailed back out to sea to learn more. We left the family nervous behind us. We sailed for an hour and found nothing.

But then, through the telescope, I saw what looked to be a ship. As we got closer, I saw that it was indeed a ship and it was English! But what could it be doing out this way? We watched the men on the deck closely and felt they were honest men. We returned to tell the others to get ready to meet them. Our family was full of joy. We dressed in our best, got our boat ready, collected fruit as a gift, and sailed out to meet the strangers.

Soon, we were in front of the ship and the captain spied us and waved us aboard. We all tried to remain as calm as possible, but it was no use. We were clearly amazed to see civilized people once again. We were not sure how to behave. The captain invited us to his cabin and asked us to tell him our story and how long we had been here. He had thought the coast was uninhabited. We told him our story and of our adventures and he was amazed to find out we had been there for thirteen years. And, when we told him Jenny's story, he jumped up.

"You must accept my welcome," he said. "One of my reasons for coming on this trip has been to find Ms. Montrose. I was sent by her father, the colonel. You must be our guests on board the ship!"

"There is a family with us, the Woolstons," he told us. "You must meet them! Mr. Woolston is quite ill and has been told to settle somewhere new to live. He is my second reason for this voyage."

We got back into our boat and both vessels sailed for the shore, where we greeted the Woolstons as they got off their ship. It seemed strange and wonderful to arrive on this land that had been ours alone for so long and to be with another family on the beach. They were happy to meet us, but their joy was nothing compared to our sense of amazement at being able to welcome the first guests ever to the land of New Switzerland! We spent an afternoon entertaining each other with tales and getting to know each other, making everyone feel at home and welcome.

That night, my wife and I talked in private. There was something I wanted to tell her that made me feel very nervous. After so long on the island and after more than a decade of work, I felt that this was my home. I had no need of a rescue. I was a happy man. I had no wish to leave this place and I told her that I wished to stay on New Switzerland. It truly was now my home and I hoped that she felt the same. I was relieved to find out she felt exactly as I did. We hugged joyfully, happy to be in such harmony. We waited until the next day to see what our boys felt about the idea and we decided that if they wanted to leave, we should tell them that they were free to go.

The next morning, the captain brought the ship around to Safety Bay so that we could bring his crew to Rockburg to show them our home. Fritz and Jack went ahead to make everything ready. As the ship arrived, the boys fired off the guns at Shark Island in salute. Everyone on board cheered.

At dinner, Mr. Woolston told us about his desire to settle in a new land because of his health. He said his sleep the night before was one of the best in recent memory and that this land amazed and intrigued him. I extended my welcome for the family to stay here and to share our wonderful island of New Switzerland. We told them we would love the company and that they would find the island plentiful and welcoming. Mr.

Woolston leaped up to embrace me and we laughed and cheered for our new friendship and for our good fortune.

"Hurray for New Switzerland!" everyone yelled.

"Hurray for those who stay here!" said Ernest, telling us by his cheer what his decision would be.

"What about those of us who are going to England?" asked Jenny.

"Yes, what about us?" said Fritz. I knew then that he was leaving, and I saw that he would be happy.

"Cheers to you!" I said.

"I will stay," said Jack. "With Fritz gone, I will be the best rider and the best shot here!"

We all laughed at this and I asked Franz what he wanted to do.

"I am the youngest and I think I should go to old Switzerland and go to school. But I will return when the time is right." We all clapped at this and thought it was a good plan. We were all going to be happy.

We spent the next days preparing those who would stay and those who would leave. The Woolstons and their daughter were to have a home here and we all discussed how the captain would tell people at home of our land. We knew that new settlers would then come to our land to make it a true colony. It was all we could dream of.

Before they left, Fritz told me that he wished to marry Jenny and I told him he had our love. I had a long talk with each of my boys and told them I was proud of them. Now we would be known in Europe and everyone would hear of our little colony.

And that is how our adventures were and how we came to be the settlers of New Switzerland. It was an incredible time for us, the Swiss Family Robinson.

I asked Fritz to take my journals to be made into this book to give to young people everywhere. I want them to know that a family can be happy together, no matter where they are and what they have. Together, we made our home and our place in the world. With family, we are never alone.

What Do *You* Think?
Questions for Discussion

~∽~

Have you ever been around a toddler who keeps asking the question "Why?" Does your teacher call on you in class with questions from your homework? Do your parents ask you questions about your day at the dinner table? We are always surrounded by questions that need a specific response. But is it possible to have a question with no right answer?

The following questions are about the book you just read. But this is not a quiz! They are designed to help you look at the people, places, and events in the story from different angles. These questions do not have specific answers. Instead, they might make you think of the story in a completely new way.

Think carefully about each question and enjoy discovering more about this classic story.

1. As they are leaving the ship, each member of the family grabs supplies that they think will be important. What would you take? What do you think is the most important item to have on a deserted island?

2. When they first land on the island, the boys all seem angry. How do you think you would feel in a similar situation?

3. Papa has a lot of knowledge that helps the family build a life for themselves. Do you have any knowledge that would be useful on a deserted island?

4. How does Ernest keep the animals from crossing the bridge? Can you come up with

THE SWISS FAMILY ROBINSON

another way to keep them on the family's side of the island?

5. Why does Fritz adopt the baby monkey? Have you ever had a pet? What kind of animal was it?

6. When the children go off alone, Papa is always worried that they are in danger. Do your parents react the same way? What is the most dangerous situation you've ever been in?

7. Papa says that the wintertime made the family feel like prisoners. Have you ever felt this way? Why were you cooped up?

8. The family builds different kinds of homes all over the island. Which home would you most like to live in? What kind of home would you build for yourself?

9. The family celebrates their first year on the island with a competition among the boys. Who did you think would win each event? What sports do you like to play?

10. Were you surprised that half the family decided to stay on the island? How did you expect the book to end? What would you have done in their position?

Afterword

by Arthur Pober, EdD

❦

First impressions are important.

Whether we are meeting new people, going to new places, or picking up a book unknown to us, first impressions count for a lot. They can lead to warm, lasting memories or can make us shy away from any future encounters.

Can you recall your own first impressions and earliest memories of reading the classics?

Do you remember wading through pages and pages of text to prepare for an exam? Or were you the child who hid under the blanket to read with a flashlight, joining forces with Robin Hood to save Maid Marian? Do you remember only how long it took you to read a lengthy novel such as *Little Women*? Or did you become best friends with the March sisters?

Even for a gifted young reader, getting through long chapters with dense language can easily become overwhelming and can obscure the richness of the story and its characters. Reading an abridged, newly crafted version of a classic novel can be the gentle introduction a child needs to explore the characters and storyline without the frustration of difficult vocabulary and complex themes.

Reading an abridged version of a classic novel gives the young reader a sense of independence and the satisfaction of finishing a "grown-up" book. And when a child is engaged with and inspired by a classic story, the tone is set for further exploration of the story's themes, characters, history, and details. As a child's reading skills advance, the desire to tackle the original, unabridged version of the story will naturally emerge.

If made accessible to young readers, these stories can become invaluable tools for understanding themselves in the context of their families and social environments. This is why the Classic Starts series includes questions that stimulate discussion regarding the impact and social relevance of the characters and stories today. These questions can foster lively conversations between children and their parents or teachers. When we look at the issues, values, and standards of past times in terms of how we live now, we can appreciate literature's classic tales in a very personal and engaging way.

Share your love of reading the classics with a young child, and introduce an imaginary world real enough to last a lifetime.

Dr. Arthur Pober, EdD

Dr. Arthur Pober has spent more than twenty years in the fields of early childhood and gifted education. He is the former principal of one of the world's oldest laboratory schools for gifted youngsters, Hunter College Elementary School, and former Director of Magnet Schools for the Gifted and Talented for more than 25,000 youngsters in New York City.

Dr. Pober is a recognized authority in the areas of media and child protection and is currently the U.S. representative to the European Institute for the Media and European Advertising Standards Alliance.

Explore these wonderful stories in our
Classic Starts™ library.

Great Expectations

Greek Myths

Grimm's Fairy Tales

Gulliver's Travels

Heidi

The Hunchback of Notre-Dame

Journey to the Center of the Earth

The Jungle Book

The Last of the Mohicans

Little Lord Fauntleroy

Little Men

A Little Princess

Little Women

The Man in the Iron Mask

Moby-Dick

The Odyssey

Oliver Twist

Peter Pan

The Phantom of the Opera

Pinocchio

Pollyanna

The Prince and the Pauper

Rebecca of Sunnybrook Farm

The Red Badge of Courage

Robinson Crusoe

The Secret Garden

The Story of King Arthur and His Knights

The Strange Case of Dr. Jekyll and Mr. Hyde

The Swiss Family Robinson

The Three Musketeers

The Time Machine

Treasure Island

The Voyages of Doctor Dolittle

The War of the Worlds

White Fang

The Wind in the Willows